# Soulless: Letters to a Narcissist

Rowan Knight

Published by 22 Lions Bookstore, 2019.

# Table of Contents

# Title Page

Soulless: Letters to a Narcissist
By Rowan Knight

Published by 22 Lions Bookstore and Publishing House

# About the Publisher

About the 22 Lions Bookstore:
www.22Lions.com
Facebook.com/22Lions
Twitter.com/22lionsbookshop
Instagram.com/22lionsbookshop
Pinterest.com/22lionsbookshop

# Introduction

The eternal quest for love can lead to happiness and pain at the same time. It seems like all the joys of life come with a price when we open our heart. But there isn't any challenge that is too big when our soul isn't too small, and it's in love that we truly test our limitations. In our aspiration to experience love, we fight, demand, persist, but also dream, feel both the good and the bad within us and others, and ultimately change our nature. The eternal quest for love is as old as the one to find ourselves, because it's in love that we can find the greatest insights to whom we are and why we are as we are.

Also in this story, these letters describe emotions, perspectives, insights and an analysis of the situations. They also promote a better understanding regarding the dynamic involved in difficult relationships, as they present dates and events organized as occurred in real life.

Another topic that is subjacent to this romance is spiritual possession, and the real dilemma that a woman experiences between loving a Christian and keeping her pact with the devil and all the benefits that come from it, and that she would lose by loving such man. The woman portrayed in this story is a nymphomaniac that sold her soul to the devil in order to maintain her life of lust, power over men and perpetual pleasure, and the purpose of these letters was to save her and save a very unique relationship.

# 1<sup>st</sup> Letter - You're Included in a Choice

**06** **October 2009 - 16:29**
I made a choice in life and, because of that, I was put in the most suitable place I should be. I have no doubt about it. For the first time in my life, the path that I have to take is very clear. But I'm refusing to walk it because I like having fun in my own illusions and abilities. And so, everyday, I get lessons that cut my ego by its roots. Like I've said before, I lived too fast. That was my life philosophy – to experience and expand. But, of course, sometimes we burn out, if we live like this. Other times, we have to use people in order to achieve what we want faster. Either way, I was playing a game that isn't mine. But now I reached what could be a new path, after obtaining everything I wanted and know everything I desired.

Everything that is happening, since I arrived to this country, is making me confront myself. But this is happening in a very clear way, as it's all connected to the exact part of me that needs change the most.

You are definitely part of that change. So, you should never feel sorry for nothing. We are what we are and things should be as they should be. Sometimes our role in someone else's life happens in a way that we couldn't predict. Sometimes we are taught by those we should be teaching. And other times, we experience in-between events what we call real experiences. So I never refuse myself anything that I believe I should accept. That is why I like so much to talk to others. I'm never exactly talking. That's why I'm easily stopped, if I'm led into dead-end subjects. And when I write anything, like this letter, the same thing happens. I'm not just talking by myself but creating bridges and exchanging emotions, among other things I should not say.

If sometimes I look unpredictable or strange to you, that is only because my life experience as taught me to do that in order to live life more peacefully. The truth is that I treasure people that can express themselves freely. So I feel myself attracted to things that just are what they are. That is also how I like to be.

I hope we can talk more often. It's interesting when you repeat what I say or answer before me things that I thought only I knew.

Yesterday you smashed me against a wall of dead-end conversation. Because you didn't say from the beginning why you wanted to talk about religion, and I never cared about what people are thinking, becoming usually focused on myself. After that experience, I could not "tune-in" again so easily, but that's ok. I value silence as much as conversations. Sometimes I speak for hours without a break. Other times I like to be alone. And sometimes I also like to be in silence among others. But since I came to this country I'm not so much like this anymore, I just follow whatever happens. And yes, just like animals live. So, it is kind of easy to smash me against "walls", as I just don't care about the future anymore. Things keep happening, and certainly much more will, as I'm only here for three weeks. But I play with other rules,... and because I should not say more for now, please answer when you can! When you wish to talk, just call me! And next time, try to have normal things to drink at home like orange juice, and not vinegar!

# 2<sup>nd</sup> Letter - Why I Don't Understand You

**06** **October 2009 - 20:30**
I don't quite understand why you describe yesterday's nigh as a "weird situation", as you didn't spoke too much. Everything you said was very normal to me. I just didn't know that you know what you know. But if you had told be before, I wouldn't speak anything and I would probably not freeze as I did. I would just be happy for that and keep talking, as I don't see anything strange in everything you have said.

Some things that you said, I have already realized it before. That's why I was joking with you all the time. I wasn't sure if you knew yourself enough. Most people don't. So I approach what is positive in this way. But I can also see everyone's weaknesses. I just don't touch them.

I believe that you live in a big castle that you don't want to leave, and that's ok. Just don't use your immense intelligence in a negative form of actions and thoughts. That is what scares me in you. I'm afraid of fear, especially in very smart and capable people. And you have fears in you. Let them go! Or at least try, when you're with me, please!

# 3<sup>th</sup> Letter - You Shouldn't Assume

**10** **October 2009 - 14:34**
It's definitely much more interesting to see your emails next to you. I'm glad my internet connection was not working this morning.

I'm not afraid of you. Well, not in the way you mention. I'm ironic in most of the things I say and I put too much energy on the words. Don't take it so seriously. I'm just an artist, crazy in the way I feel and express. I like you the way you are. If you pretend to be someone different, I'll feel uncomfortable and avoid you. I just never expected to find someone like you in my life. I'm paying back a big value for this experience. That's why it's being so hard on me. I didn't expect it.

As I've told you, I came to this country to play stupid with life, not to have my spirit completely burned to ashes. That is what is happening in many different ways. I feel like I'm burning from inside. And I'm trying to deal with this the best way I can. But I feel trapped most of the times. That's why I feel pain. I've learned to live life in a completely different way, and so, for me, all this experience here, you including, feels like a rebirth. I feel like I'm dying at the same time. Don't take it personally. Be what you want to be, feel what you want to feel and say what you want to say! What concerns me, is for me and only me to solve. So, let it burn!

I like you very much and I love our conversations. Don't assume so many things! But say whatever you want! I'm addicted to experience. So, don't worry about me. I hope I don't make you feel bad in any way. Sorry if I do stupid things sometimes. I'm just lost. I've played too many games and now things are happening to me in a very strong way. It's easier for you if you to just think that I'm crazy.

**ROWAN KNIGHT**

My house is a mess, just like my head right now. So I don't know when I'll be ready to invite you for a tea. You must wait!

# 4<sup>th</sup> Letter - Misinterpretations

**13** **October 2009 - 02:02**
I forgot my work at your place, but it's dangerous if I go to your house in the morning or afternoon. I won't be able to leave easily again. So, I'll just try not to forget it tomorrow night.

Sorry for the kiss at the front door, but I merely took yours in our first time like this as an open path. Either way, I think it doesn't matter anymore. I never wanted to pressure you into anything, but I wished this moment for a long time, and I'm sure you too. Maybe you just didn't thought it could be like this.

There are no barriers in my mind or in my reality. I just follow energy. You can block that energy, but not with words! I can feel what you feel and know what you think, so be honest with yourself and you'll find the right way! Pain can only come from contradictions. Solve them and pain will go away! We attract everything that we have in our life, but we always have a choice when dealing with it. I hope you can sleep well tonight!

# 5<sup>th</sup> Letter - Our Confusion

**18** **October 2009 - 09:31**
I grew up in violent cities and with tyrannic parents. I spent most of my life in confusion, trying to understand why I was so different. Adaptation never worked, simply because I couldn't understand things that people just do by instinct. So I spent all my life studying human behavior. With seven years old, I was already writing papers by myself, full of descriptions about different people that I knew. I would analyze those papers to see differences, common attitudes, changes of behaviors and permanent actions. But that personal study wasn't enough. My religion was also not enough. So, as a teenager, I rebelled. I chose anger, instead of sadness.

During that time, I was reading a lot about psychology, including recorded interviews with patients, trying to understand what is behind human behavior. And I used that anger, by being with groups that supported it and respected it. My life at that time was all about fighting, making people feel stupid and controlling them. But it was still not working for me. I still didn't felt human and I felt that I wasn't doing what I was supposed to do in my life.

The next step was to understand who I was. I went inside dozens of religious groups. And, step by step, the pieces started to match. As these pieces matched, I started to change, I was seeing more and realizing more about myself.

This path was always very difficult, as I was forced to accept the truth about who I am. I had to accept things that nobody ever told me, but where inside me already. That is the reason why I studied so many religions. I was trying to understand who I was and what my purpose in life is.

That change was very difficult, but made me more of who and what I am. That is why I was able to fix my life and win all the challenges that were put in front of me. I discovered my true personality and what I could do with it. I also found what my purpose in life is and how I should live it. And with that, my level of happiness grew like never before. I started to smile more often and I started to be able to make jokes about everything. Now I can smile all the time because I feel at peace with life.

There were many people in my past that helped. Some of them were exactly like me and where able to show me things that I didn't knew at that time. I had to study all the information very carefully and test it in my life to see if it was really true.

I was only able to be free and happy once I sopped avoiding that truth and simply worked with it. Once I did, everything else followed.

I understand that, since we met, you're afraid of the things I can do. At the same time, you're trying to end this fear by changing me. You think that you can change me by making me more like everybody you know.

I'm sorry to tell you, but it won't work! You can't make me have abilities that I wasn't born with, things that I could never understand, because I don't have them and never will!

I spent my entire life trying to understand myself and my reasons to live. It was also too difficult for me. But I was able to find happiness and peace after I did accept the truth.

I've tried to make you feel happy and wild, because I cannot do that. I cannot lose control. I can only feel the same things through you.

If you refuse what I am, you are refusing me. Don't expect me to loose control, don't expect me to reject the connection that I have and allows me to have a never-ending vital energy, don't expect me to feel things that I cannot feel, and don't expect me stop having things that I have now! If you don't love the person I am, you don't love me.

What you did yesterday was a rejection. I love you. But our relationship won't work if you don't love me. I told you that the only way to end this relationship was if you chose to do it.

I guess you're choosing it that way. Yesterday I felt rejected. I still love you too much. I still cannot be without you. I still wake up thinking about you. Each day that passes, I love you more. But each day that passes I feel more rejected by you.

If you want to have a normal boyfriend, that does normal things and feels normal human things, good luck in finding him! I'm not that person. Think about what you are ready to accept before saying sorry, and then make me feel the pain of rejection, as I feel like a monster every time you do it!

I'm just a living being, like you. In my own way, I live, just like you. Love it or reject it!

I love you, but what you did to me yesterday was a destruction of what exists between us. I can't kiss you or be next to you anymore!

I really tried to be at that dinner-party last night, but I couldn't look at your face and I couldn't pretend to be happy. If I had been there, I would have done many bad things to many people present.

I don't want to feel anger or do bad things to others, so I decided not to go.

I want you to know that I still want you in my life. I still feel the same way I always felt about you. I still feel pain when you're not with me.

I never felt with anybody else what I feel with you. But you have to accept me as I am! I won't be happy if you don't. I will feel miserable, if you keep trying to make me become something I'm not.

You have to put your past behind and accept me as a new experience in your life! I'm not your ex-boyfriends, I'm not your mother and I'm not your friends or your family. I am what I've told you that I am. I have nothing to hide. But I have plenty about myself to make you understand. I cannot be with you, if you reject what I am. And you're not helping me if you do that. I can deal with many things in your life and inside you, but if you reject me, the relationship cannot exist.

I'm giving you time to think about all this and understand what you really feel towards me. It can't be just your strong heartbeat when I'm close to you.

# 6<sup>th</sup> Letter - Your Dilemma

**18** **October 2009 - 18:30**
I don't know what to do with you. You keep insisting in avoiding the roots of the problem, which is you always trying find a way to do one of two things, put me out of your life, or transform me into someone you can feel more comfortable with.

Maybe you changed your apartment so much because you cannot change me. I tried to have patience, but you keep doing it over and over again.

I still feel rejected. I still feel that you don't know me and don't want to.

How can you expect me to change simply by touching my hand? Especially, if you don't say anything. It's like you're making me feel stupid.

I want you in my life but not like this. It's not about the mistakes you make. It's about the origin of all them.

I don't know what more to say. I'm watching you playing a theatre created by you and that you don't want to leave.

# 7<sup>th</sup> Letter - How I Can Help You

**18** **October 2009 - 20:00**
I can help you. Don't be afraid, please!

You're not weak, and I never though, and will never think, that way about you. You cry because you're strong, you can feel.

I'm not throwing knifes at your heart. That is an illusion made by your subconscious against you.

The roots of your nightmares are connected to the things you love the most. That is why you're afraid to be happy. That's why you think that I'm hurting you. That is not true and you know it. I was too strong and too direct again. I'm sorry! I feel threatened by what you have inside and that fear makes sense, especially after you said things that have hurt me a lot, like yesterday. That is why I came so strong.

I don't like to feel fear. I attack when I'm threatened, just like you do. But I'm not attacking you. I'm attacking what you have inside. The pain that you feel exists because you don't want to be free of that thing.

I can promise you that I'll be more careful next time. But the main thing you must know is what we feel about each other! That is what matters the most.

Give an opportunity for our relationship to grow, like I've been doing since the beginning! I never stopped, even when you hurt me. And yes, I felt my anger disappearing when I looked at your yes and touched your hand today. I just had to be certain that you wouldn't do the same thing again. That's why I had mixed feelings and that's why I waited for your actions and words.

I couldn't stop thinking about you all day long and I miss you.

I'm too strong and demanding with people, but I'm even more with myself and the people I care.

# ROWAN KNIGHT

Please say something! You're just making me suffer more and now you've put yourself into it also.

Don't feed the pain when there is something beautiful growing!

# 8<sup>th</sup> Letter - I'm Not as Patient as You

**18 October 2009 - 22:08**
Today I was eating dinner at the canteen and saw two men cooking next to one another. One had his flame very high, practically up to his face level. The other had his flame at the minimum. But both finished cooking at the same time.

We had three problems in just one week, one after the other. The flame is high, but I believe that in the end the result can be the same as those two men.

I told you that I was prepared to keep the flame on, no matter what happens. And you promised not to have radical attitudes again. Today I gave you an opportunity for us to talk, even if I wasn't feeling well, but you aren't doing the same.

I'm not as patient as you are. I can't just be quiet. Tonight I won't be able to sleep.

I'm doing for you what I've never done for anybody else. I'm fighting to keep you, no matter how painful that can be to me.

Due to your reaction to my email, I now understand what you've done yesterday, and, at the same time, I also understand why you feel as you do now.

You don't have to feel this way! You don't have to fear me or take me out of your heart! There's no reason for that. Don't be the stone you asked me not to be! You're much more intelligent and mature than that.

# 9<sup>th</sup> Letter - Unconscious Cruelty

**24** **January 2010 - 21:07**

Don't destroy this relationship! Look at what we have, carefully!

Maybe one of your friends have said to you bad things about me or the relationship, or maybe you're just afraid of having a real relationship for the first time in your life. I don´t know the reason. What I know is that you're destroying the beautiful relation that we have.

I don't want to give up on you but you're leaving me without a choice. I´m very sad and hurt, as I truly want to love you and I know you're the one I waited all my life for.

If I feel this, you must feel the same. Don´t ruin our life! Give us as many opportunities as you can! Help me in dealing with the problems! Answer the phone! You are destroying so much...

Why do you talk to me about hate when you're the one destroying beautiful things such as our life together? Why do you talk to me about love when you're the one closing your heart? Why do you talk to me about being careful not to lose what we have, when you're the one giving up?

I'm very hurt, as I gave myself completely to this relationship. I moved all my things to your apartment in the first weeks without thinking twice.

I forgot the pain once I saw you in France. In one morning we were talking about having our own house, having children, working together in another country and, basically, being happy together. At night, on that same day, you finished everything. Why do you give so much pain to yourself and me? Why can´t you just accept love in your life?

I really want to build a life with you because I love you.

If you don't want me anymore, at least help me in dealing with this pain in a less painful way, because it seems that this breakup is much simpler and less painful for you than for me, for reasons you must understand for yourself!

# 10<sup>th</sup> Letter - Love Shouldn't Be Difficult

**03** **March 2010 - 16:50**
Loving someone shouldn't be so difficult.

I'm seeing you creating a distance between us that tends to grow.

Every time my hope grows, you steal it. Every time my heart opens, you crush it. Slowly, step by step, you're letting die what we had.

I don't know what to do anymore. I can only watch what you're doing, as I have already done everything I could.

It's sad to love someone that can't accept love.

No wonder people don't believe in our relationship. You don't behave like you have one.

We agreed not to talk about the relationship. I did it. We agreed to talk only when something was wrong. I did it also. And what should I do, when you decide to disappear like you don't care about me or us?

Personal problems are never an excuse to disrespect another person, especially, if you're in a relationship with someone that cares. I don't think I deserve such behavior. I don't know why I waste so much time writing these things. You don't care, and even if I say it face-to-face, you don't understand. I don't deserve this for sure.

# 11<sup>th</sup> Letter - Your Decision

**10**<sup>**March 2010 - 11:23**</sup>
You may have acknowledged that you refused love, but you're not recognizing that you still do. Life is not about what you lose, but what you choose to lose. When you refuse the "present", there's no gift to be kept to enjoy the future. Apologies don't erase the past and show no hope for the future.

I really want to believe in us, but I cannot believe in the "us" alone, as the "us" is made of both you and me. If you act looking only at the "you", the "us" will slowly die.

Every mistake you do to the "us" hurts me, because I feel it as if it was my own. If you fail, I fail, because I also want to believe in our love.

Understand my words as help for your own consciousness.

To believe in our restart I cannot see the same behavior pattern over and over again. I want to keep being proud of having you in my life, so please act differently from your past experiences, by simply accepting what you wish!

I don't want to talk about our relationship again. I just want to believe in it.

# 12<sup>th</sup> Letter - Our Breakup Doesn't Have Winners

**12** **March 2010 - 10:53**
In a breakup, there are no victories, only losses. You've played defense too much in our relationship. That attitude led you to always see my words as attacks, even though they're not. I was hurt by not having your love, and only that. That is what I expressed. The more I wanted to love you, the more you pushed me back, and then I've hurt you with my words because I was in pain.

I'm not a person that hurts others, and the most difficult thing for me was always to hold my emotions and words. But, as we aren't together anymore, I would like to be your friend. I don't know if I can, but at least it's a way to make the breakup less painful.

I didn't want the relationship anymore since our last breakup. It was your touch and kiss that awake everything inside me. But I wasn't the same anymore. Your email helped me to believe again. You used many beautiful words and a complete honesty that made me feel very proud of having you in my life. But once you pushed me out of the house that night, I started to close again, as I lost my trust on you once more. Now, I'm completely close. Nothing will make me want to be in the relationship again. But I will like to finish this properly. We can talk normally. We've done that very well in the past, before the first kiss.

You are a beautiful person and this is why I was with you. I told you this many times. I could see all the beauty inside you, even if you couldn't. But as love is the only thing that I wish to have at this stage of my life, I pushed very hard to free you from your shadows, so that all that beauty could be free.

You saw it with me many times. But I wasn't good enough and failed, and I'm sorry.

At this moment, I only wish that both of us can find happiness and peace. I wish you a good life and, no matter the problems we faced, I really loved our moments together. You are the most interesting person I've known in my life and the only one that allowed me to be myself, completely free to be who I am. And I thank you for that! It was an experience that changed me deeply in a very good way.

I believe with the greatest wisdom comes the biggest change. The biggest transformations are always more painful, as they change the safest and deepest structures of the personality. Because of this, I'm not sorry for the pain that the relationship brought me. I'm only sorry for bringing you pain.

In the end, I saw true love and experienced it. Only for that, waiting a lifetime was worth it. I feel blessed because I've seen love with all my heart. I don't know if I can find it again but it was worth to experience it.

Please be happy! It's the only thing I wish for you. I will be in peace if you can.

# 13<sup>th</sup> Letter - Your Contradictions

**06** **April 2010 - 12:49**

When you called me nine times, crying and at 2am, I took you in my arms, because I didn't want to leave you alone in your pain. But you abandon me all the time.

If you love and you abandon the person you love, you don't love yourself.

Love is not what the movies show you. Yes, love is perfect but not as you imagine it. The perfection of love comes with the pain of accepting it. It means to accept another person in our heart as if that person is our heart itself. It means the risk of high doses of pain in order to achieve something higher even than our souls.

To be in love is to have a powerful fuel in us, making us go faster in the path of life, finding happiness, the purpose of life and, ultimately, who we are, because the one that loves can see everything.

When you hurt me, I wait or avoid you, until I'm able to deal with the pain, because I know that you do it due to your own illusions.

When I hurt you is the same. I don't try to hurt you on purpose. When I avoid you, is because I'm in pain. When I'm in pain, I cannot talk anything to the person that has hurt me.

After all that you've learned, after knowing that in that afternoon you rejected me and I, in pain, searched the company of a friend, making you feel abandoned, after knowing that we behave differently according to cultural principles, after knowing all that, how can you just end the relationship and break a promise? What kind of person are you? You knew that your behavior wasn't justified and you still did it.

I waited for you in the restaurant until 3 o'clock, even without knowing if you would come. Later, I saw my colleague by accident and went for a tea with him. You saw us from the window by coincidence. If you hadn't I would call you later to take you to a restaurant, as I didn't felt like cooking for you after what you did. But because you called me and acted like you didn't want to see me anymore, I decided to bring you dinner. I arrived at 7pm. A good time to eat dinner, don't you think? But you had already gone crazy and run into a hotel in the middle of nowhere. When I called you, everything you said was full of anger, as if I was your enemy.

If I'm your enemy, you have no friends. Only someone that could love you so much could take as much as I took and always come back with the hope that you could be a better person, while feeling joy when you felt better about yourself.

On the phone I asked you not to breakup. The next day, I waited for your changes. The only thing you had to say was "I will keep my promise" or "I don't want to break up with you". Only this would be enough, but instead you broke-up.

What do you expect from me? You're playing with me like I'm your toy.

I know I hurt you but I never did it on purpose. When I'm hurt, I avoid that person, but eventually I come back. But you, you just breakup.

I never breakup with you because I respect you and I respect what I feel. I cannot breakup with a person I love, even if I'm hurt, because it doesn't change the emotion. I cannot live in the fear that the person sharing life with me may leave me. How can I build a future with such a person? You cannot even keep what your promise and then you say you love me. If that is true, then you don't love yourself.

I could take that pain away but you've put me out of your life. I won't give you another opportunity to do it again. I could ask you to promise but you cannot even keep your own promises.

As you have seen before, I don't demand much from a woman. When I love, I truly commit myself. It's sad not to find in life someone that could just believe in this and accept it. That woman could be very happy in ways that she couldn't imagine. Maybe one day.

# 14<sup>th</sup> Letter - Giving Up on Yourself

**08** **April 2010 - 06:52**
In some days the pain defeats me, and those are the days in which I think that I can give up. I get burned out from all those rejections of yours. Then, the love I feel for you changes the negative feelings into positive again. I get crazy with wishing you since I wakeup until I go to bed everyday, and it's an emotion that becomes stronger and stronger. Not even two months apart where enough and you know that it's the same for you.

It's not me that you're giving up. You are giving up yourself, because I just want to love you.

We are the same and we react in the same way. If I don't talk to you, you'll feel the need to come back to talk to me. You know it! Just as me, you have days in which the pain in unbearable. Just as me, sometimes you just want to give up and then, you realize you can't because of what you feel. And, just like me, you believe that finding each other was the best thing in our lives.

How can two intelligent persons with all these answers just give up? We know that everything that happens isn't our fault, and we also know how to make the relationship work. And nonetheless, we give up on the only thing people search the most in their entire existence: Love.

For me, life is about loving someone that can match us perfectly. And I found that person in you. That is why I'm with you for so long after what happened.

Don't give up! It's because people made you believe that we could fight all our lives that you give up. It's because people believe you need things that you don't see in me that you give up. There are many people making you feel confused, and for this reason you make such mistake.

Your neighbors fought for three years. Imagine that! We don't have to fight not even one more day as we have something so special.

I cannot just stop writing, because what I feel for you is very strong. I love you and I want you back. The only person that couldn't make me feel pain is the person I cannot love, so it's not your fault as I just love you.

We didn't met by accident. There was a purpose. If you don't believe, remember all your life before coming to this city! I didn't choose to love you. I just do since I saw you. And I'm not writing to push you to anything or hurt you. I just miss you very much.

When I talk about love, I just talk about what exists, without giving any credit to myself. What exists is this:

- We both wished to meet each other;

- We both lived difficult months before coming here, in which we wished to have love in order to keep moving through the hardships of life;

- We both wished someone that could make us feel happy and fulfilled;

- We both wished someone to share a life of dreams and built a future of hope;

We got all this and it couldn't be more perfect.

The pain comes from the inexperience of never having it before and, at the same time, as something in the way to make us learn how to respect one another in order to love more.

As I told you before, it's just a wall of fire, and that's why we are where we are, and have what we have. On the other side of this wall, everything is beautiful. Love is what allows crossing those changes. Without it, humans cannot just do it on their own. What we have is a gift, and comes only once in a lifetime. If I was the one coming to your life, is because I'm the one that can help you with what you want. The same applies to me.

Think about what I wrote! It's not about the words but what you can feel through them. Don't give credit to me! Give it to your heart! If I'm right, it's only because I follow the truth, the same truth you can reach.

You have helped me a lot in dealing with my problems, and it's thanks to the relationship that I can do so much.

I'm sorry if I've hurt you or not trusted you enough. But everything came from the fear of losing you, the same fear that you have regarding me. It's because we love each other so much that fear exists.

It will go away in time, as perfection doesn't come in an instant. It's built, just like a sculpture. But the one that sees beauty, can find it in a rock, and make something beautiful out of it, as beauty was already there.

We have made ourselves into rocks but we've also built the beauty that was inside with the relationship. We don't need to ask anything from each other, as love builds it for us through what we already have. It's because I can see the beauty inside you that I can love you and the same applies for you, and that's how we change. But we don't need to decide to change, just love. Time and life will do the rest.

These last two weeks were perfect. It was the fear of losing ourselves that ruined everything once again. It started in the day that we talked about going out of this city to find another job.

Do you know why I reacted that way last time you breakup? Do you know why I said that I never wanted to see you again? Do you know why I seemed so quiet? Because I have the fear that one day you may leave me. I did it because I want your happiness.

I know that you need me out of your life to find the job you want in the city you've chosen without attachments holding you, I know that this is what made you think so much about the relationship in the last days and say things that made me feel hurt. It's because I knew this that I avoided you, as I didn't know what to do.

I want your happiness, but I also love you with all my heart and, for this reason, I tried to let you go. What I said was to let you go, so that you could easily do what you want to do with your life. This is the whole truth that I didn't want to share before, because I didn't know how to say it or even if I should. I wanted to let you decide for yourself if I'm worth to be part of your life.

Sometimes the pain of respecting your decisions is unbearable but I do my best. Like I've said, it's the fear of losing you that makes me feel the need to protect myself. When I pushed you those days, it was because I needed proves that you want me in your life, just like you need romanticism as a way for you to know that I love you. It's because I love you so much that I've hurt you.

I'm sorry! It's not about trusting you as much as it is to fear losing you. You are the most beautiful person that has ever entered my life. If my only goal in life is to love you, I'll be much happier than with anything else that I've ever achieved.

# 15<sup>th</sup> Letter - Unfair Game

**17** **May 2010 - 06:12**
It's very painful to believe so much in a person like you without any expectations besides love. It's the only thing I ever expected from you: Your love.

You've expected much since the beginning, and at the same time, you have contradicted yourself completely since then.

I believe that you've built a perfect world inside you that you're tremendously afraid of losing.

I was surprised and amazed about how much you could help me in the last weeks, but I'm very sad to see how easily you still give up all the time.

I'm caring for you in a different way than what you expected, but I tried to express it in the way that you need. Once I did it, you found another excuse for your sadness.

I forget what brings me pain and I remember what brings me joy. The more disappointed you felt about what I forgot, the more I did it. But I believe that it's not fair to be expelled from your life because I don't remember the things you need me to remember in the right time. It's not fair to ask me to stay when I want to go and to ask me to go when I need to stay. It's not fair to give your body to me when I need your love, It's not fair to pity me, but, above all, it's not fair for you to embrace so much pain believing it's the right thing to do.

You said to me, just two days ago, that I think too much with my brain and that this is the problem, that you work with your heart and I don't. But you're the one finding justifications and reasons to breakup while I just open my heart to you all the time.

# 16<sup>th</sup> Letter - Difficult to See

**25** **May 2010 - 07:45**
You say "my colleagues are going to pick me up" but it's always only one and the same.

It's as difficult for you to see me with my Spanish friends as it is for me to see you with yours, because they will do their best to put us apart (it's in their nature to do it, as it benefits them), and I can see it in their comments. All of them, when talking to you, have power in their words:

- "He looks nice without the undertaker coat", seems like a very naive comment that works in your head this way: "He is a wolf dressing now as a sheep"; and you behave likewise, expecting something bad in my words, no matter what I do or say. You expect the wolf inside a sheep;

- "I have an American friend that was cheated by a guy from his country" works in the brain like this: "These people are not trustable, so I shouldn't expect anything, because sooner or later it's going to end dramatically";

- "People from that country are very dumb", made you stop asking for my opinion, which is the opposite of what you did in the beginning, when we could learn together, because if people in my country are dumb, your brain says to you: "I shouldn't expect knowledge from him"; so you just do all the learning on your own, including the learning of my language, what you could do with me.

It's interesting the fact that people use different phrases according to whom they're talking to. Some may say to you: "I was fighting with my past girlfriend for many years until we breakup". Because they know what you fear the most is to fight with me all your life.

That same person knows that I don't fear that if I love, so he or she will use a different phrase for me: "My girlfriend was so used to fight me that she always found a new reason to do it until she met someone else". Because they know what I fear isn't the fights but the lack of will to finish them and losing the person I love.

This is to say to you that everyone has weak points that are easy to be reached by those who need to do it for their own benefit. When we touch, we know the main truth: Our feelings are real and true.

There are things that I don't know how to express to you, because I don't want to hurt you. I need to express more when I fear the coming of problems and I fear them more when I feel you in anxiety.

These latest months have been very difficult and we need to talk more and more openly, but I'm being careful for the reasons I've mentioned and others. First, because you're not super strong as you want to believe. And second, because I love you and I only care about your happiness. Therefore, I'll express concerns only if I feel that rocks are blocking what we both wish to accomplish together.

# 17<sup>th</sup> Letter - What You Feel

31 **May 2010 - 12:26**
I understand how you feel, but that doesn't make your actions correct. What you feel is very normal and everyone has problems in their relationships. Only those that don't feel anything for each other will behave in a way that will show no difficulties to understand and pass forward. Like you, I also have the right to feel bad with words and actions. I believe the solution for this is to talk about it and move on, otherwise it's not about us but each one of us, as the reasons will persist inside ourselves. But we don't create problems. We awake them. If we love for the first time, we awake deep emotions for the first time as part of growing. The solution isn't to disrespect each other by avoiding conversations and seeing that this brings more pain for the future, because we both know it's not what we want.

This week I'm here but next week I'll have much less time again. Let's not waste it! I'm giving opportunities to us. Don't behave with me like I'm just another man in your life, because I'm sure I'm not to be compared to the others you had!

Every time you do that, you keep behaving in ways that I just don't understand, as they don't match the way I behave. I don't function like you but I know you. I'm speaking these words for you to understand; I'm not playing games. I'm very serious when I go talk to you. I hope you understand this soon and I hope you can just help me stop what started yesterday.

You said that you love me. I love you too! This is enough for me if it's enough for you. Because I believe that with this comes the rest. That is how much I believe in you and us. Try to respect it, please!

# 18<sup>th</sup> Letter - The Need to Control

**31** **May 2010 - 13:35**
In the beginning you finished our relationship many times and then you said sorry. After finishing it you came crying to keep it. Then you spent two months treating me like dirt and saying that you didn't want the relationship anymore.

When you went back to this country you where so afraid to lose me that you called me everyday. I came back to you because I believe in you and because after everything you did, crazy or not, I still love you.

In this country, again, you ended the relationship many times. When I started to be apart, you tried to win me back and, if you couldn't, you would starve and not sleep. Then, another fight came, this time bigger, with physical aggressions from your part, but when I lost my job you realized you could lose me forever, so we went back to be together. With the new opportunity that I received, things seemed stable, so again we had more fights, but because we didn't spent time together you wanted to finish the fights quickly. Now I have one week free and you finish the relationship in the first day, ironically, after saying you didn't expect anything anymore and didn't want me to leave; Also, after starting by saying, and I quote "I want to leave you but I can't".

You can believe that I'm analyzing you while I believe that I'm trying to understand you, in order to be able to see how you want to be loved, because as the fights continued, so your motives changed every time I fixed the problem.

- 1st we fight because you're afraid to lose me;

- 2nd we fight because you think I'm ashamed of showing an older girlfriend to my family and colleagues in the campus;

- 3th we fight because I complain about your behavior all the time;

- 4th we fight because you believe I want to change you;

- 5th we fight because I don't listen to you;

- 6th we fight because we fight all the time (humm, confusing, isn't it?);

- 7th we fight because I feel insecure in the relationship (and wow, this took two months, maybe because you're so afraid of losing me, I believe);

- 8th we fight because you believe I'm aggressive and can hurt you (interesting, as you're the one that has been physically aggressive, and apparently, according to your own words, not for the first time);

- 9th we fight because I say bad words to you;

- 10th we fight because I don't express (Wow! What a change!);

- 11th we fight because you think I'm not romantic;

- 12th we fight because you think I'm not caring;

- 13th we fight because you're unhappy;

- 14th we fight because you think I'm unhappy;

- 15th the relationship has become so silly that now you fight with me when we don't kiss.

But yes, we've been very happy. In the days you believed we could be happy without a fight. In those days, dreams were becoming reality because we both didn't want to fight.

I've tried to show you that many times but you're too afraid to believe in it. For you, a relationship is a war about control (and I wonder who were the previous idiots that screwed your brain regarding loving in life), so you're afraid to be controlled and in need for power all the time. Then you got surprised when it doesn't work as you expected and you say the other person is confusing.

The first day we kissed, you didn't want to kiss me. I thank the door that didn't open for the kiss I didn't want to take by force. In the second day, when we were dating, you wanted to end the relationship.

I'm not judging you because I love you and I know everyone can do mistakes. I'm also not perfect and I can hurt, just like you. I can understand that you had a very difficult life and, at the same time, I also understand that it's because your life was so difficult that you have learned to survive in an uncommon way, which allows you to be the best in some things and the worse in others.

I admire what you have achieved in your life and I admire your courage in life, dedication to work, and will to succeed. When I met you was like a dream coming true. Even better than that, as I was so amazed with the fact that we were a perfect match. I was too much excited over it and allowed myself to go with it without thinking twice. I did for you what I never did before for anyone.

Then I saw you using your intelligence against yourself. I tried to help and my help turned against me, as you blamed me for making you feel bad. But I have learned a lot in this relationship from many different sources. I've connected what I already knew and, when I saw my predictions coming to present, I knew that my theories were correct.

I helped myself as much as I could and I changed a lot in order not to give you pain anymore, but if your pain doesn't find match in my actions, finds it now in my inactions. So, if I kiss you but don't ask what you did during the day, or if I ask it but don't kiss you, or if I ask about today but not yesterday, or if I simply forget, anything is a valid reason to blame me for your unhappiness.

I'm not an analyst and I'm not a psychologist. I just observe. I feel what I see and in the feelings I receive the answers.

You even believe that flowers can survive with me for an entire month or more, in opposite to the fact they die with you after one week, because they absorb my negative energy and live from that. It's amazing to see how much you change reality to match your needs! You need to believe that I'm the source of your pain and you need to believe that we will fight forever; you need to believe that we can never be together.

I've let you go as far as you could inside me and I've helped you to be as happy as you could be, but instead of using it to believe in me, you've forced yourself to believe you're unhappy. And is it because of me? You're unhappy, but not because of me. Remember your words weeks ago: "When all those students loved me, I felt a huge emptiness inside and a lot of pain. I believe I started to realize it with you as in loving you I realized I had pain inside me".

Do you remember what I told you? I said: "It's by keeping yourself loving beyond that pain that the pain transforms into love".

Far before this happened to you, I already knew it. It's the pain of being exorcised into true love. The light always creates pain. It's the pain of exposition. When we expose our weaknesses, our rage, our deepest thoughts, we feel fear. Fear comes from experiences of pain, and pain means death. So, if the one that brings light brings pain, the light becomes death for the one in pain.

The most amazing achievement in life comes when we can love beyond the pain.

You gave me pain because you felt pain. I gave you pain because I felt pain. This cycle repeated itself until I stopped it inside me, as I wanted to love you beyond the pain. When I managed to do it, you runaway because you felt alone in your pain.

I'm not giving you pain. You feel pain with me for other reasons. The truth is that, if you can handle the pain, it will decrease the power slowly in time, until you feel no more pain. In that moment, you'll easily see our relationship with joy, have fun with it and feel blessed inside it. This is a universal fact that I'm sharing and prove is there to be seen. Our relationship has become better but you live in contradiction.

I've only asked you one thing during all these nine months: Don't break up with me. What did you do? You started doing it almost everyday. Then you became afraid of fights you create yourself.

Yesterday I gave you a choice once again, and once again you've chosen the negative action.

I expected you to do something different for nine months and I would have respected you if you could keep the relationship for at least one month without saying "I quit".

I don't know how much more I can love you. It's not when you give me pain with words that you hurt, but when you give up. I don't believe in you wanting to give up but you need me to believe it. The thing is, if I do, you'll not see me anymore.

I've given you proves of that before and that's why you couldn't reach me anymore after coming back to this country in February. One day, life will put a big barrier between us and, in that day, even if I want, I won't be able to do anything anymore.

It has begun, as I lost my job here, and now I see you only on Mondays and Thursdays. Could be worse; could be better. Your thoughts and actions are creating it. If you don't want me to believe in us, the process will continue. It's how life works. As for me, I'm accepting that, but I want to love you at the same time.

I'm sure you wouldn't be so open if I'd breakup with you thousands of times, if I'd said I didn't love you for eight months, saying that it's some crazy feeling that will disappear or just something that we brought from past lives.

What I'm doing today, once again, is helping you awake for what we have as long as time is at our side. If you cannot see it, I'm very sorry and goodbye!

Eight months to accept that you love me. How much more time and pain to accept that you want to love me?

I feel alone and in pain as I care about you and I gave myself completely to the relationship to prove to you how much I want you in my life. After all these proves, it's like they have no meaning to you.

# 19<sup>th</sup> Letter - Not Because of Me

**07** **June 2010 - 07:10**

This relationship was hard on you but not because of me. Our relationship is gold. We've got everything to create anything. But you put apart this amazing opportunity of life.

I could respect it but I can't erase the feelings I have, as they're stronger than me.

I don't ask you for anything! I feel with you and it's too strong. Stronger than what I can handle. So I prefer to have pain than to put this love apart from me. Even if loving means having pain, I choose to love, and if you leave me, you leave me, if you hurt me, you hurt me. So, do what you want, but I'll not block my heart!

Hell and heaven may go inside me to create a huge war. I don't care! I'll open my heart to you until I have no more strength inside myself. I choose to love with all the consequences of it and I'll not give up loving.

Travel to another planet if you want, stop talking to me if you want. I will love you until the end.

The pain I feel in this relationship is the pain of faith, for seeing beyond reality. You stay in the pain but I'm looking ahead of it. I'm not supposed to accept your decisions because they're not your decisions and one day you'll realize it.

It doesn't make sense to write anymore if you don't read it or if you'll read whatever you want in my words, but I want to tell you this:

- I know why we have fights and you know it also;

• I never said bad things to you but you don't want to solve your own problems, so you'll always read what you want without knowing the exact purpose of the texts I send you;

• Something has happened during our vacations apart in January and February and if you're breaking with me it would be fair if at least you tell me everything, instead of just blaming the relationship;

• You may feel too much remorse and resentment to go back to the relationship but you can do it if you can forgive yourself, as I did forgive everything all the time;

• You know that the only way to solve your life, including your health problems, is by accepting love and loving openly without expectations. You may choose to start from level zero with another person but life doesn't work this way and it's a very selfish attitude that you'll learn in the future by having others doing it to you;

• I know that you can go back because I know how you went this way, but it takes time. You cannot deconstruct in one day what was built in nine months;

• I'm not asking you to come back to me. I'm asking you not to give up on us, not to give up on life.

You're playing too many games that will turn back on you. You enjoy seeing me sending a lot of messages because it makes you feel more wanted but one day it will stop.

It's not wrong to see me and kiss me but it's wrong when you pretend you don't want the relationship. You lie so much that I wonder if you can see what truth is.

Know this: Every time you lie to someone, you'll find a reason not to see that person, as seeing him confronts you with your own guilt. So, when you don't have a choice, you'll find something to justify the lie. If the other person is mean to you, the lie is justified and your conscience gets free. That's how easy it is to blame the non-guilty party and end a relationship.

You cannot take it anymore because so many lies have made it unbearable to accept it. The conscience of evil is too heavy, so you need to blame in higher levels.

You can go so far in this attitude that you even change roles. Yesterday, for example, you decided that it's me that cannot receive love.

You've never stop surprising with such an imagination. If you could just admit all the bad things that you've done, our relationship would get back to 100% and the amazing thing is that I can forgive everything; besides, most of them I already know. For example:

- Nr.1: You never went to buy the tickets for our holidays;

- Nr.2: At least one night, you stopped my breathing to wake me up because you couldn't sleep;

- Nr.3: Long ago, when I was seeing my bank account, you spied on my information to see how much I have in the bank;

- Nr.4 Many times, you have seen the files in my computer.

What I'm doing when I ask you for simple things like this, is not to judge, but you're too much afraid of everyone. You believe that you're independent but you're not. You're just lonely and comfortable with loneliness. You may be very intelligent, but it's worthless as your brain loses too much energy in self-protection and lies. You're too afraid of losing yourself but an amazing world would open for you if you could.

I'm giving you what I see in order for you not to lose so much time in your life anymore. I believe you're too much inside your own mental games and, when you find someone like me, being honest and talking what he thinks, it becomes confusing to you.

You can play games for the rest of your life but I don't see the purpose of that.

It's important for you to make me believe I'm wrong but I'm not. You change your mind like the wind changes its path, so I would never go with you to another country without a job. How can I risk my life with a person that breaks apart a relationship in less than one week, every week? I believe that it's fair that you go away because I couldn't give you what you want. You want a man at your feet, luxury and independency without any responsibilities. Interestingly, you also desire a kid, but if you cannot commit to a person, how could you commit to a child? Could you love this human being forever?

I gave you all my thoughts and you hide yourself as much as you can, so, yes, this contradiction would never work. As one week ago you made me feel like a prostitute, I guess you took your revenge on men by using me. I'm glad I could help!

When I met you, I saw a scary girl that wanted magic love with a sword and a shield. You may think that you're an independent strong woman but it's not what I see. I see a little girl with an helmet, sword and shield, searching for love in a battle.

You may create all the stories you want about whom I am and why you left me but one day in life or death you'll see a truth you could never imagine.

Meanwhile I would appreciate if you didn't hate me, use bad words to describe me or make me feel guilty for your own decisions. Nobody lives forever but I'll die with a clean conscience and karma about all this at least.

# 20<sup>th</sup> Letter - Hoping that You Find Peace

**08** **June 2010 - 14:08**
May you find your peace and happiness as I'm now learning to find mine!

You broke my heart more than thirty-eight times in nine months, so I don't think I can feel it anymore.

I don't breakup because I respect you. When you breakup with someone you hurt a lot the other person and it's not fair. Besides, being hurt isn't a reasonable reason to end a relationship but you're too immature to understand this. You breakup with me in an average of once a week. That makes it thirty-eight times in nine months.

You've reproached me every time I tried to talk to you about what is happening, for helping you, for trying to understand the reasons for our problems. Do you really believe I don't accept responsibilities? Or do you need me to feel guilty to let yourself have a lighter burden?

You say that you've helped me write more, and it's true that you've helped me a lot with my writing in the beginning, but you also said that I just "play with words", that I "waste my time instead of working for the classes", that is "worthless to work for something that brings no money back", among many other things.

I don't blame you for influencing me in stopping the writing; I know that in the beginning you did the opposite; But you never believed in my abilities or knowledge, and you've put me down many times using what I write about.

You say that you're trying to keep the relationship but are the breakups every week your way of saving the relationship? Is it reproaching for every little thing, including the ones in our distant past, your way of helping us?

Don't say that I took your hopes and faith as it's because you never had them that you could not handle the relationship. You're not able to love and that's why you cannot feel joy with me. Every time that I have joy, you break it; Every time we're perfect, you find a reason to destroy our perfection.

The reason for your lack of joy is inside your head, not inside your heart, and for sure it's not to be blamed in the relationship or me. It's with me that you woke up for the real joy. Go read the email you sent me after the breakup and go out with the new Spanish teachers to have fun and maybe try to change boyfriend as you decided that night that there was none in your life. In that email you confess that the reason for your lack of joy is your own past and the fact that you cannot accept love.

You believe that our relationship is over until despair takes power on you and you see that the truth of life is beyond your decisions. It's in these moments that you receive the biggest pain and the worse diseases. You should know it by now!

You've never truly looked into my eyes, because the feeling you awake when doing it is too strong for you.

I wish you could say "thank you" instead of "this relationship is over", because it would clean your soul, fix every problem and allow the flow of love to keep moving, instead of opening the gates of pain and sorrow. I also wish that you could accept my apologizes every time I offered them, because it would bring forth the same effect as yours, instead of playing the strong woman that is superior to every man on earth, and making me say "please" for loving you and wanting to be with you.

It's because I believe in my happiness with you that I've stayed with you for nine months. Not for sex, because the more you attacked me, the less I felt physically attracted to you. Only love was there with the same strength all the time and this love made me happy.

You say that if I've made you feel as you're the most precious thing for me you would make me feel the luckiest man on earth but I did it and it didn't work. I understood with you that too many fulfilled demands spoils a woman and makes her more arrogant and selfish. So my theory now is that a woman that cannot respect me shouldn't be with me.

I thank you for caring about me and I wish you had done this before, instead of reproaching with hate and making me develop fears I didn't have.

I did my best to love you and I'm sorry to have failed. I don't regret loving you as it wasn't a mistake, but I regret that it didn't work as I've dreamed it would.

# 21<sup>th</sup> Letter - What You Want to See

**15** **June 2010 - 13:52**
It's important for you to believe that this relationship would never work, that we both contributed for the destruction of it, in order to be conscious free and guilt free, and move on with your life without the pain of regret.

I can help you by giving you many theories proving what you believe and even building a logical prove saying that I'm a very dangerous and an evil person. It's quite easy to do it! But it would not make it true!

You may keep searching the internet for information and other theories that prove what you want to see but you see what you want to see and if you believe that it's true, it's true for you!

You're a very lovely, strong, motivated and intelligent person that deserves to be happy and in peace with life! Don't blame yourself for what happened between us! Was it real love? Yes. It didn't work? Yes. Leave me in the most peaceful and gentle corner of your heart and I'll be at peace with everything that we've experienced in this relationship! No matter what, I'll keep good memories of you!

# 22<sup>th</sup> Letter - How You Broke Me

**03** **July 2010 - 12:36**
Suddenly, everything made sense and even if everyone, including you, was telling me that I was dating a crazy woman, for me, there's no insanity without a logic that has produced it and is able to do the opposite, by bringing the situation back to sanity. This logic was missing, to match all the pieces of the puzzle. I was sure there was someone in your life but I couldn't imagine something like what you've told me. I couldn't believe it but it made sense. I just had to wait for you to say it.

During all this time, even if you didn't say it, all your behavior proved that to be true. Including when I looked into your eyes and asked the truth about why you wanted to be in another country, far from me, and you lied with all your body and the tinniest muscles.

Before meeting me, you had plans to move to France and get married, but because you had a stroke everything changed, so you needed to rethink your life. You moved to a new country for that reason but you didn't expected to fall in love for another person – me, and, as you still had plans to get married, you've hurried up in stopping our relationship the next day after it started.

The confusion of feelings made you stay in-between, and the need to hide it made you create problems, in order to make me be apart from you. You needed excuses to go away as your feelings didn't let you do it. You needed proves that I was a bad person to clean your guilty conscience. And for that, you tried everything. For ten months many reasons have been taken into consideration to analyze me, but I was too good, as you didn't receive any bad reactions, not even a slap after kicking me dozens of times. This made you completely mad as it increased the amount of guiltiness inside you, not only for what you did to another person but also for what you where doing now to me. You had heart problems again and death knocked on the door once more because when you hurt a man of peace you hurt yourself with a disease. It's the will of the soul to leave a guilty body, to leave a mind in pain. You can call it fate, but there's no fate without a path.

Maybe going out with other men is normal to you and maybe being apart from your lover also, but it was by doing this that you've destroyed a future marriage.

I don't want to be the second one to go through that experience and, as you've done to others, I believe you can do it to me. You've hurt me enough and I'm not a merchandise to be compared to your ex-boyfriends or to wait for your approval.

You said one day that my love for you would change. You made it change, as you've entered my life and became my world, and in ten months transformed my paradise into ruins.

You can't see it, as you still behave as always, but I'm not the same anymore and I don't look at you as before. You will never have me back with your arrogance, superiority in behavior, sex appeal or whatever you may still believe is working with men or me.

The only way for me to believe in you again is if you become completely honest but with so many lies how can I trust you? You've even said: "I don't believe in honesty. Honesty is not good". How is it possible to build a future with someone that says this? In all of your messages saying...

- "I hope you are ok";
- "I'm worried for you";
- "Good night".

... I wished you could have opened your heart and say:

- I love you;
- I don't want to lose you;
- I'm sorry for what I did;
- Let me stay with you;
- You're the man I want in my life.

But you cannot do it. You try to make me come to you instead of lowering your weapons and just knock on my door as I did to you so many times.

I have put my ego apart for you all the time but you can't do it for me. In your selfishness, you expect me to do it all the time.

As you lie so much, I don't look into your eyes anymore. I wanted to believe in you and I gave you ten months of my love but you've used it with no consideration for my feelings or respect towards me. You've remembered me in your loneliness only and you've put me away anytime you felt like. You show no respect for life.

I believe in universal truth, I believe in honesty, I believe in eternal love and I believe in complete happiness. I believe that life has given you a second choice but you're too much inside your own pride and selfishness to see it.

Save money for your wedding and get married with the one brave enough to wait for you for so long as he'll give you the happiness you're able to handle! I won't wait for you like the others in your life but I'll remember you forever. Maybe we'll see each other again in the next life and then you become my wife.

# 23<sup>th</sup> Letter - What Love Is

**08** **July 2010 - 21:43**
Today you asked me: "Do you love me?" If I said "yes" I would have shown me a job you found in the neighboring city, next to you, but because in your pressure with a nonsense question I said no, you decided to tell me that I would lose you and the job you found, as you would never tell me about it.

Do you really believe that this is the way to respect the person you should care about? When you love, you don't ask to be loved back and you don't blackmail your partner for love. You have no idea about what is love and then you blame others for what you do, a manipulation in which you put the other person down without any consideration for his feelings or life.

I won't change just because you want. Don't give me more pain before you go away just because you're in pain yourself! You cannot demand love and you cannot come to my house and ask: "Do you love me or not?"; "Will you forget the past?"

I spent eight months with a person that said she didn't love me and I've loved you with all my heart, without expecting anything in return. I was respecting you, even if I believed you loved me and where too afraid to admit it.

You want me to say "I love you" in three days of pretending to be someone you aren't, after I've loved you for ten months until you killed all the emotions inside me.

You're unable to respect my feelings or assume your responsibility in this situation. You just demand all the time. You believe the whole world exists to serve you and even love should be available when you want but it doesn't work like this. Love may have come to your life but it's your responsibility to keep it and nourish it and what you did was the opposite.

You had a person worshiping you with all his heart and eyes on you and you have fought for ten months to kill it all. Now you demand this love to come back just because you want it? It won't. You must make it grow again from the root of the huge tree that you've destroyed and wait. It takes time and patience as it's much easier to destroy, even if this three was so big and strong that took ten months to finally be cutdown.

As I told you before and many times, by keeping putting us apart, life would put us apart so much that, even if I wanted, I wouldn't be able to do anything to fix it. This is what has happen! Nonetheless, the barrier that you've created isn't only in being apart but also inside my heart and my brain. With all your manipulations and lies, with all the breakups, the pain transformed my brain in a way that is much harder to overcome than I could ever imagine. You've given me so much pain that I'm completely ready now to let you go. After so much of "it's over" and "I don't love you", what else could be new? I gave you all my love with all my heart and my life while you put me away and kept saying "I don't love you".

I've chosen not to stop loving you, so life, in order to protect me, did what nature is supposed to do by changing my nature. The love for you changed. You've decided your life, found a new job and sent your things by mail to the new place where you're going to live. In the end, you want to bring me like I'm some kind of furniture.

You've put me in last all the time and you still do. You've planned your life without me. You've disrespected me completely, you've said the worse things you can say to a person that cares for you, you've put me out dozens of times, you've said that you didn't love me hundreds of times and, basically, you've made me suffer a lot for loving you. There're things that you do that are very mean and I would never do.

I would come to your place and say: "I love you, and I want to be with you. I would be happy if you accept this work in the city where I'm going, even if we aren't together, as I enjoy your company very much and I'll keep dreaming until the day we're together again". But instead, you used this as a play card and in the end of pretending to have changed, it was like you were saying: "You don't say what I want so I'm going to make you feel pain! Look, I had this for you and now I don't give it to you!"

This is very sad for me to see because makes you look very selfish and rude. It looks like you tried to manipulate me and it also proves that you're always trying to control me and punish me. You're revengeful to the person you should care about the most. I would never plan any revenge against you and it's sick even to think about it.

There are things in you that I would never do because they're not in my nature. I would never repeat your behaviors to make you feel the pain you make me feel and I would never manipulate you to see if you trust me or not. By making me feel anger (when you put me down) and pain (when you send me away) all the time, you made me a very sad person.

Do you want a miracle now? Don't ask me. Pray! I hope you can find your happiness and, if possible, the man of your dreams!

If, as you said, I'm the only one that has made you react like this in a relationship, it shouldn't be difficult to find someone that can make you react normally and in this way help you be happy.

# 24<sup>th</sup> Letter - I Won't Say

**09** **July 2010 - 11:42**

I won't say anything anymore and I shouldn't have said anything before, as you can only give me love when I'm in silence and only when far from your life it becomes an evidence. Between the bitterness of my presence and the love of my absence, I choose to be remembered and forgotten, like a flower that has shown love and with it has rotten. Go in peace!

# 25<sup>th</sup> Letter - Self-Destructive Logic

**11** **July 2010 - 19:31**
You seem to have a very good self-destructive logic, eager for knowledge that can strengthen the source of this uniqueness and in this way create an illusional safeness that leads nowhere.

In the end, knowledge can be resumed to a simple purpose: Either you do good or bad with it. If you're not happy with the result, it can't be good. If you believe it brings you happiness, all I can say is: May you be happy without me!

To be right may be the most important thing for someone that has been wrong many times; To believe that mistakes make sense may be the most important thing for someone that has suffered a lot from them; But truly, the most important thing in life is to be happy, and this means admitting we've been appreciating the wrong road, as we didn't knew any other.

It's easy to find imperfection in what is perfect but the thirst for imperfection comes from a mind unwilling to see perfection because it reinforces itself with imperfection as a way to create more reality in its unique world.

We always get more of what we see. Your need to be right will put you away forever but you'll keep fighting for it until the end and this will give you a meaning to live, even if illusional. One day, out of despair, you'll find a theory that proves the non-existence of love or soul-mates, in order to get peace and you'll have it, without love!

There's no sacrifice in what has an important meaning beyond the sacrifice itself and this you'll never understand. In using what you know about my life against me you created your own cage of pain and this is why you're suffering and with lack of peace. It's the inability to properly listen to the heart.

# 26<sup>th</sup> Letter - Until Death Breaks You Apart

**12** **July 2010 - 09:38**
You've proven me that my behavior was correct, and that once again you tried to manipulate me, this time pretending to be a nice person that you really don't want to be.

I was happy with the woman I saw the last days, until the moment she demanded my love as a price to pay for her efforts, as she didn't do it out of her heart but necessity to control my emotions.

Seeing how much you put your pride and need to win in front of something as deep as mutual emotions, makes me feel sad for you, but, at least, even if you can't love, you've received it for ten months.

You shouldn't have reacted like this towards my openings yesterday but it's in you to win till death breaks you apart, among many other key-ideas and key-phrases in your subconscious mind that I hope you can find, understand, and erase, in order to stop sabotaging your own happiness. I hope you've learned something out of this relationship that can be used to help you and your life!

Your attitudes show me that I'm behaving the right way, so all I can say is goodbye and good luck!

# 27<sup>th</sup> Letter - What I Want

**12** **July 2010 - 15:19**
Do you really know what I want? Maybe it's much simpler than what you think; Maybe it's so simple that you really don't need to do anything about it, as it may very well be what you also want. If you believe that life has to be hard, you'll lose the beautiful things from your hands just because they're simple. I'll tell you what I expect from a woman in love with me:

• Commitment: She'll never give up on me, even if she feels pain or anger. She will never breakup with me or avoid me because of painful moments. She'll find a way to deal with them and solve it inside the relationship so that one moment doesn't destroy everything;

• Persistence: As she believes in our love, she'll try to be with me as much as she wants, without playing any games. She won't give up;

• Clear words: She will say "I love you", "I miss you", "I want to be with you" and not something in-between;

• Respect: She will not play with my feelings by testing my reactions to her provocations, even if she is an insecure person and needs it. Instead, she will respect me and trust me. If she has doubts, will ask questions. She won't provoke me all the time and hurt me just to get the information she wants;

• Honesty: She'll say the truth and expect me to do the same;

• Common Plan: She will do her best to live with me and create a common life, no matter what happens;

• Golden Rule: She won't do to me what she doesn't want me to do to her: Jealous attitudes; competitive behavior ; hiding plans; etc.

If I see all these things, I'll marry her for sure, because I don't need much beyond love. Just to know that this love is working. If you think about it is what I did for you all the time:

• Commitment: I never broke up with you and I always tried to overcome my feelings on my own. After that, all I wanted was to be with you and I wouldn't give up until I had you in my arms again, no matter what you said; For me love is total commitment for life and I may seem old fashion but I can do it and as so I demand it;

Persistence: After all I did to be with you, there should be no more doubts regarding this issue;

Clear words: I was always very clear about my feelings towards you;

Respect: It's difficult to respect a woman that finds pride in saying that she had many boyfriends and fucked a lot of men just for fun, among many other things that you do and say but I respect who you are and I made efforts to understand you by asking the questions I needed and by believing in you beyond what hurts;

Honesty: I try very hard to say the truth and to say everything but it's hard to do it with someone that believes that holding information is an advantage;

Common Plan: You always decide your entire life without asking me any questions and in the end you expect me to understand it.

You may be seen like having attitudes of an independent woman but independent women end up alone. That is why they're called "independent". I'm the opposite, by always trying to make plans for both.

You may be feeling sad or lonely but the fact is that you don't plan with the other person. You behave in a very selfish way.

- Golden Rule: You should think about what you've done and said if it was me doing it to you! You can learn a lot from this exercise.

I believed in you but I don't know how much you believe in yourself because in fact you met a very healthy person that makes you feel the need to destroy him in order to find peace in yourself, as he makes you feel out of peace, but love is about changing the inside to create peace outside. If you do the opposite, you'll find yourself without love. It's a choice, so I'll finish with a question: When you die, what was the purpose of your life?

# 28<sup>th</sup> Letter - Lies

**11** **August 2010 - 14:59**
The lies that have destroyed our relationship are the reason why you feel like this.

In many moments you've blamed me for things that I haven't done and in many moments you've confused me inside your own confusion. You've played with me for your own entertainment. You'e entertained me to entertain yourself.

In one day, you reproach me for not being caring enough, in another day you say that I don't pay attention to you, then you reproach me for not being romantic and, among all justifications, you act with the least justifiable action of all: You leave me.

It's not only me that you are leaving. You are abandoning mostly yourself.

You said that you love me, you said that I'm the man of your life, you said that you wanted to be with me forever, you said that our relationship was different from others you had in the past. If that is all true, why do you leave me? Why do you leave yourself?

Even sex became an argument for complains. We went from you saying that I was the best lover you ever had to saying that sex with me wasn't enough to please you. Where does the lie stops or starts?

You've lied about so many subjects that none seems true anymore. Nonetheless, the biggest lie of all is in you deciding to leave me. Leave me or yourself? Who are you really leaving?

You've said that your previous relationships have been better than this one but you've also said that I've been the best thing happening in your life. What kind of thing are you talking about after all? Are you insane or am I too stupid not to understand you? Do both possibilities exist?

You're a liar and lies have destroyed our relationship. Why should you say now the truth? The only truth I can see in you all the time is the same I saw the first day I met you: You can't love. You are able to destroy and maybe you've learn to love it. You can love pain.

I remember the confidence and smile you've shown, barely hiding it, every time you've caused pain. You may lie about this, but you can't avoid the fact that you've hurt me many times, whatever reason you may give to it. Every criminal can justify his behavior, at least, with his insanity, but there's no greater criminal act in the world than to refuse love.

There's nothing more beautiful in the world than the unification of two beings that complete themselves when together because in this union they find their true home, inside and outside their hearts.

You're the light of my world, the reason for me to live and the reason why my love flows in a never-ending stream. I could leave all my life behind just to have one kiss from you.

You've refused happiness when refusing me. You've gained a lot from me and you've learned a lot, but when there was nothing more to receive, you got bored and you've blamed me for being bored.

Today you despise me and say that I've made you unhappy. It's true that I've wished for your happiness and I was unable to achieve it but I wonder if anyone has ever done it. Is happiness in you or me? You've said to me full of certainty that to love me was not enough. You said that happiness is more important. So, I ask you: What greater happiness is there in the world besides loving someone?

You've said that I love you more than you love me. I disagree. I believe I can accept our love more than you. Or maybe I let you love me more than you let me love you.

If love isn't enough for a human being, you believe we should wish what only a god wishes – the peace of nothingness. But you're human, so in fact what you are wishing is death.

## SOULLESS: LETTERS TO A NARCISSIST

It's not my love that you refuse; you refuse life because my love has increased your faith in happiness. I've not betrayed you as much as you've betrayed yourself because, in all the mistakes I've done, I've never abandoned you. You've forced me to leave you because you can't recognize that I'm your life.

The shadows of death obscure the clarity of your thought. From nothingness you came and to nothingness you shall return. You're a suicidal person with a heart jumping for survival, a living dead calling for the hope that you can't really see.

In me you found your destiny but, as you've never seen it, you couldn't recognize it. You dream now to have a different reality but I'm your reality. By running away from me you'll find more of the same – your sadness and emptiness; and in that pain you'll find your image – the vampire wishing for what she can't have: feelings.

I know today that I only needed one thing to rescue you: make you happy; but is it possible to make a dead person feel alive? What I say always has your support, not because you believe in me, but because you want me to believe in you. You say that a certain sweater doesn't look good on me but if I choose it you answer: "I know. I wanted to see if you could see it too." You make me believe that you're offering me things, when in fact is just an emotional trap to ask in return. You suggest for me to spend vacations with you in the city you're going to work and when I say yes you suggest the opposite, because in fact you want to see where I'm going and spend vacations in a new place. You're a manipulative selfish woman.

If you trick me two thousand times and I don't trust you, you'll say that you can't behave properly because I don't trust you. When you create a fight, you expect me to react. If I say something, you avoid me and then you reproach me for not kissing you and hugging you. You put me down by saying that when I write books I'm just playing with words, that what I write is a copy from people's ideas or that I'm just inspired and nothing is mine. You say I shouldn't write if I don't feel pleasure and that when I write I don't experience life. But you're envious because when you started to write yourself you said to people I was also a writer without telling them that I've written about love. You prefer to say that I've only written about educational subjects because in doing it you set yourself free from responsibility. You're dumb, stupid, envious and selfish!

# 29<sup>th</sup> Letter - My Eternal Love

**19** **August 2010 -17:48**
I've loved you like I've never loved anyone in my entire life. I've loved you so much that my body reacted as if it was facing death every time you said goodbye to me. I loved you more than I love my family, to whom I said goodbye for years without thinking twice. I've loved you more than my friends, to whom I've not even said goodbye to. I've loved you more than I loved myself, and for that I woke up from a long deep depressive sleep.

You've entered in my life like an angel and in that day I felt like the luckiest and happiest man on earth. With you I felt accomplished in life; I felt that I'd found my soulmate. You helped me find joy in life and meanings to live. There were no more doubts in my life. I was in the right path. I wanted to marry you as soon as possible and start creating a life together with you. I was ready to have children with you, build a dream and bring it to reality. I was completely inside my dream with you and I was loving you with every single little cell of my body. Then, you said I was suffocating you with my love and that was the first huge pain that I received, as I couldn't give you love in the same amount that I felt it. After that, you started rejecting my love in many different ways, each one of them so painful as if someone was taking the best part of me. From your mouth my heart suffered the attack of many arrows:

→"I don't love you";
→"Soon this love will disappear";
→"All my ex-boyfriends were better than you";
→"You make me unhappy";
→"I don't trust you";

→"You're violent and aggressive";
→"I've lied to you, I don't care about you and I never loved you";
→"You killed my love for you";
→"You're not the man I want in my life";
→"I prefer to have a simple life than to have love";
→"I prefer to have a caring man than a loving man like you";
→"You're immature! I want a real man";
→"Your help has hurt me";
→"I look like a dead person thanks to this relationship with you";
→"This relationship is making me very sick";
→"Like mine, your love for me will transform into something else";
→"We will both find someone to love and that's the best for both";
→"If I stay with you I'll be unhappy all my life";
→"You're evil";
→"You're mean";
→"You're a liar";
→"You're greedy";
→"You're weird";
→"You're stupid";
→"You're just like my mother, who has given me the biggest pain";
→"I'll always hurt you and I will not change";
→"I'm going to another city and I don't want to see you there";
→"I'm going to another country and I may not see you again";
→"I don't believe in this relationship anymore";
→"I will be happy but not with you";
→"I want you to find someone else to love".

Physical violence was also for sure a big arrow in my chest, especially because you justified it with my words, although you've always shown aggression in many other forms.

If you believe physical aggression is excusable, you should ask the ones that have been aggressive to you in the past for their reasons as I'm sure everyone has his own motives.

You've always been unhappy with me no matter what I did and the reasons for your rejection were always different:

→"You don't know how to make love to me";

→"You don't care about me";

→"You're not romantic";

→"You're not interested in my life";

→"You're too self-centered";

→"You don't care about my problems".

I understand that, in the end, you tried to change your behavior, but you couldn't. You didn't put me out of the house anymore but in another form you found a way to put me out of your environment all the time. You kept the lies and the manipulations and that's why I felt myself going down in my lack of hope instead of up, as I saw no reason to believe anymore. The continuing of your behaviors allowed me to understand you profoundly as you're only surprising for those who don't know you enough or aren't able to really know you.

All the experience in this relationship transformed itself into something else for sure, just as you predicted when you said "our love will transform into something else once I leave you". My love for you became an act of compassion instead of an act of giving love, as my pain became knowledge and the relationship became wisdom.

During all the experience I had with you, I managed to also create the profile of your ideal man, which I will never be and this is why I told you: "I'm not the person you want to love". These are the characteristics of the person you want to love:

• Rich – you said many times you need luxury. A rich boyfriend cannot be called greedy when he tries to save money for his own debts, because he won't save money and he won't feel bad when spending money for you and receives no appreciation about it, because he can spend all he has on you easily;

• Stupid – If he his stupid he can't see your manipulative techniques, such as "thanks to me you're more happy now", "Thanks to me you're not having miserable vacations", "I always know what's the best for you", "I don't eat because of you", "I don't sleep because of you". He wouldn't see that your control over a relationship (a control that you need because you cannot really love without fears) is based always in the same strategy: The guilt and self-respect of the other attached to your actions. He wouldn't see that you take his happiness into your world and control him by making him feel that you're the source of such happiness;

• Non-Artist – Artists are too sensitive and they feel too much the pain, so you need someone that isn't so "touchy" or "sensitive" as you say. You need someone that you can hurt without any remorse, because you can't handle other people's pain, especially if you're responsible for it;

• Low self-esteem – As you need to complain about your partner's behavior and actions without any reproaches in return, the only way for you to feel perfect in your behavior is to live with someone with no self-esteem as you can complain without feedback;

• Independent – You need a man that doesn't need you because in this way you can do whatever you want without having to explain anything or ask first; you can say goodbye and disappear whenever you want and be accepted when you come back; you can say "I don't want to see you anymore" and stop seeing him for weeks until you miss him for sexual reasons or not; and if you miss him only sexually you can use him as a prostitute and say goodbye the next day like you did to me;

• Caring – you need a man that gives physical proves of his love everyday for you to be able to believe that you are loved. He should give you flowers, bracelets, earrings, rings, etc; otherwise you won't trust his love as words have no impact on you, unless they can bring pain; so, I could say "I love you" for an entire year and you would never believe. In the beginning you said that it was a crazy emotion that would disappear, then you said I didn't love you because I didn't

touch your neck and hair often, and then you said I didn't love you because I didn't kiss you enough but, after all, you just never believed in it, except in a few moments of physical proves;

• Naive – Because every time you say "let's forget the past" he will be able to do it, he will believe you and then you can hurt him again exactly in the same way you always did;

• Older than you – As you won't feel ashamed to present him to your friends, colleagues or students. If he is older than you, you won't say that he's immature, you will not disrespect him and you will not behave with him like you're better because you have more life experience; also, you'll not feel the need to teach him anything about life as you don't like to share what you know with others, not even with the person you should care as an equal, your soul mate, your lover.

What I saw in the beginning was very clear. I never told you that you're a low level person, but you said it yourself, and it's a fact that internal pain creates external pain; it's also a fact that pain doesn't allow a person to think clearly and see things as they really are and not as they seem to be. If you're afraid to love, you'll give pain to those that love you, as you believe that they may hurt you; in hurting them you hurt yourself and create your own cycle of reinforcement of a self-belief. In psychology it's called a self-fulfilling prophecy.

I still see in you the little girl that I saw in the beginning, holding a huge shield to protect the heart in one hand and a sharp sword in the other hand pointing at all those that try to touch her fragile heart. This is your karma - your pride, developed to protect you from humiliation.

You received the biggest pain with me because pride is solved with love. By giving love, you release the ego, and by releasing the ego, you release the need to be right, the need to win, the need to protect, the need to be worshiped; by releasing these needs, you release the fear that is connected to all of them, as it was fear that created the qualities that built your personality and trapped you in this self-made armor.

The less love you have, the more admiration you need, but you refuse love by focusing in the need to be admired. This is why you work so much and feel so empty at the same time; it's the karma you've built. Just like you became the best in the need for dealing with people, you've detached from your inner self.

Through love, I've connected all the different personalities you hold into one; I've hurt your pride. But karma is a dynamic process and you couldn't do your own part because real love isn't a negotiation like what you believe; we should not love only if we are loved; we should love even if we don't receive love. Real love isn't blind; only passion is blind. And so, I can say that you didn't really love me because your love isn't unconditional; your love has conditions: my love or what you see as my love - my proves of love. It is by not being honest in love that you believe that I've lied to you. In fact, by believing I didn't love you and still don't you're just lying to yourself. Dishonesty traps you in your own mental certainties that have no connections with reality. But you expect others to believe in them. Your logic doesn't make the truth as the truth is always there to be seen.

I was blind in my love for you in the beginning; then I simply loved you as I will always love you. When we love, we don't give up until we have no more strength. But when we don't really love, we play games to see if our partner will run after us when there are problems.

Real love doesn't wait and doesn't take time to become real. I've run after you and believed in you until I couldn't do it anymore; I delayed all my life to see your plans with me, for us to plan the future together. I didn't search for any job as I only wanted to be with you above anything else. I could work anywhere and in anything just to be with you but you did the opposite; you've followed your pride instead of love. When I was in pain you secretly organized all your life the best you could without any consideration for me. Real love isn't selfish.

No sword in this world could make me stop loving you but the love you couldn't accept started killing you. When I saw your face changing into an image of death, when I saw you in a pain that made you so weak that you couldn't stop crying and feeling the worse person on earth, when I saw that you could kill yourself because of me, when I saw all that, I gave up.

I've loved you beyond any pain and in this love I let you go. I have handled a pain worse than one thousand deaths to keep the love I feel for you and I'll handle a pain worse than three thousand deaths to let you live and be happy. If I have to, I'll die to make you live. But I'll do my best to return to your life forever in every single lifetime.

Today, as I write this letter in tears, I say goodbye forever. The demons have won in my own game. Today they take my body and my brain; they take my life, but not my soul.

One day I was asked if the soul can love beyond the body. Today I know that the answer is yes. I'm not my body, I'm not my brain, I'm not my words, I'm not my emotions, I'm not my happiness and neither my pain. I'm my soul and my soul will be yours forever as it has always been.

The eyes in which you see the world today won't see me again but in your prayers, whether I'm alive or dead, I'll always be with you every time you need.

For one year you've pushed me out of your life and refused my love, despite my efforts to please you. I felt that I was going to die every time you decided to breakup. So your behavior made me face death for one entire year, every single week.

When everything was finished, you tried to recover what you had done in just a few days, but my body survived to the pain of rejection by rejecting you. I loved you beyond my body's capabilities but I couldn't behave again in the same way and I couldn't run after you anymore, as I received a painful feeling if now I tried to do what I did in the past, which resulted in a deep emotional pain every time I put myself down for you.

You could proudly say many times that you've fucked many people but you couldn't say one time "I love you too" to a man that declares his love for you during one hour completely opening his heart. You've rejected him the next day and for the following months, all the time and forever. As my words have hurt you, I stopped writing and talking, but as now even my silence hurts you I have no more ways to be who I am. Without being who I am, how can I exist with you? I can only love you.

You gave up on me but I was always there until the last minute. I was never late as my time was your time since the beginning. It was the right time and the right moment to live love. I've done all I could for you, I've endured pain since the beginning till the end; I cried many tears and I exposed myself enough to cry many more in the future every time I remember in sadness what has finished. But today I turn a page in my life. I make thirty years old and it's the most sad day of my life as I receive the loss of the biggest present I could ever have – you. Tomorrow I start a new life but I didn't choose it. I was forced to accept it as all my attempts to keep love in my life have failed. I've failed in keeping you with me but I did my best beyond what I could imagine I could do for someone.

You've been my first true love. Thank you for sharing a beautiful love with me and for helping me in this love to become a better and stronger person. I'm deeply sorry for everything that happened and created this result; I'm deeply sorry to see you in pain as a result of the relationship.

By seeing your words in the last emails you sent me before I go, by listening your voice on the mobile and observing your behaviors in these last moments, I can see that it's true what you say: You'll never change.

You pretend to change expecting me to believe in it and you believe that I don't want to love you just because I act differently from what you expect in this game. You believe that I lie when I'm being completely honest to my feelings and it's because I'm honest to my feelings that you cannot handle my behavior.

If I was pretending, you wouldn't see my sadness. I've given you many proves of my love but you can't see them.

I understand that you need to believe in your own illusions in order to protect yourself from the pain and the responsibility (or guilt in your point of view) but I hope one day you'll be healthy enough to see clearly your part in this experience and move on with your life into a better condition.

From today, I forgive your mistakes and pain as I hope you'll forgive me for mine! I release you from your guilt as I hope you can do it for me!

As a birthday gift, the most important I could receive is your happiness. Please be happy and may your wishes come true! I'll always remember the moment of my life when I saw you for the first time and, as the tears blind now my eyes, I let the sparkling magic fill this beautiful memory with which I end today my story with you. In September 2009, eleven months ago, the most amazing woman entered into my life. I'll keep this special and kind moment frozen in my memory with these tears I hold now in my face while I finish this letter and end this enchanting tale. This is the day in which heaven has blessed my life. You will always be my little angel.

# 30<sup>th</sup> Letter - Your Mind

**21** **August 2010 - 23:36**
Stop sending me messages and trying to call me as I won't forget how you've been to me during all this time, one entire year to be more precise, in which I was doing my best to be with you. I'll always remember the moments that make me realize why I want to forget you, so that my pain may shutdown my feelings towards you:

**Moment A**

YOU: You're violent.

ME: But I've never hurt you physically not even once. You did; you kicked me many times.

YOU: Maybe one day you will.

ME: Well, maybe if you kick me ten more times, one day I'll slap your face as a response to that.

YOU: See! That's what I'm afraid of. You're violent!

**Moment B**

YOU: I've forgotten all my mistakes in the past. Why can't you do it?

**Moment C**

YOU: I love you. Why it's not enough?

ME: Because for six months you said that you don't.

YOU: Why you don't believe me now?

**Moment D**

YOU: I've had many boyfriends in the past but you're the worse because you don't seem to care about me.

ME: Why do you say that?

YOU: Because this morning you didn't kiss me.

**Moment E**

YOU: I don't trust you because you remind me my mother. She speaks like you and I don't trust her.

**Moment F**

ME: Last time we had a fight you have been physically aggressive.

YOU: That's nothing. I've punched one my last boyfriends and I can guarantee you that he felt it.

**Moment G**

ME: You're very aggressive in physical ways.

YOU: It's because I feel aggression at the same level in your words.

ME: You cannot compare words with physical aggression.

YOU: Yes I can!

**Moment H**

YOU: You're mean and evil!

ME: No. You're mean and evil.

YOU: How can you say this to me? Get out of my house!

**Moment I**

YOU: You never care about me.

ME: Why do you say that?

YOU: because you never ask what I'm doing.

ME: What are you doing now?

YOU: I don't want to talk about it.

**Moment J**

YOU: You never ask about what I do during the day!

ME: I do but you don't answer.

YOU: I don't because it's private.

**Moment K**

YOU: I'm sad with you. Do something!

ME: What can I do?

YOU: I don't know!

**Moment L**

YOU: I'm nervous.

ME: Why?

YOU: Don't talk like this!

ME: What did I do?

# SOULLESS: LETTERS TO A NARCISSIST

YOU: You're starting again.

ME: Starting what?

YOU: Don't do it please!

ME: Do what?

YOU: Get out!

**Moment M**

ME: Please stop hurting my finger!

YOU: Why are you shouting at me?

ME: I'm not! I just asked you to stop hurting me!

YOU: You break my heart all the time!

**Moment N**

YOU: Why don't you trust me?

ME: Because you say "I don't want this relationship anymore" every time we have problems.

YOU: You don't forget the past no matter what I do. I don't want this relationship anymore.

**Moment O**

YOU: You have knowledge but you don't help me.

ME: I don't know what to do anymore.

YOU: But you should!

**Moment P**

ME: You're always going out with other men on your own.

YOU: But at night is with you that I sleep.

**Moment Q**

YOU: You can spend the night with me but in the morning I want you out because I don't want this relationship again.

**Moment R**

YOU: We could have been working together in the same city.

ME: You decided to choose a job without telling me.

YOU: Why do you always blame me for our problems?

**Moment S**

YOU: Why don't you talk to me?

ME: I have nothing to say!

YOU: You don't love me anymore; you've lied to me; you don't love me!

ME: For six months you said you didn't love me and now you complain about me?

YOU: I knew it! You don't love me anymore!

**Moment T**

YOU: Go away to your new job and have a good life! This relationship is over!

ME: I hope you forgive me in our love that has come to an end!

YOU: My love will never end! Never!

Please go create the next insane moments – U, V, W, X, Y and Z, with another idiot! I had enough! I don't believe in your love anymore!

# 31<sup>th</sup> Letter - Things that Change

**23** **August 2010 - 14:13**
Things change and I thought that you could see it, not as something bad, but just as a result of everything else. I love you very much but you gave me no choice! You're very dear to me but you put so many barriers in front of us that it's like you're afraid to love. You ask for my love but when I give it to you I feel you rejecting it.

All the pain that I've shown you in the letter is the pain of a man that wants to love a woman that puts barriers all the time. It's like I'm fighting to enter your heart and receive arrows in my chest every time I get close to it.

In the day that I said to you: "I'm in love with you", I started a commitment - to love you. No matter how much pain you gave me and no matter how much your appearance may change, I always loved you. In words of sadness, pain, frustration, anger or even in my silence, I'm always loving you.

You know now what you want in life. Your present job will build your pride into something stronger but you don't need it anymore! Love gives you that and much more beyond your dreams. Do you want to prove that you're a normal person? Accept Love!

I won't give up until I do all I have to do to make you accept love, but I need you to do your part! I need you to come here!

The mind is complex but also simple to understand. You can change everything inside yourself with one simple decision! Don't be afraid as you don't want anymore what you can lose. You want what you're afraid to win. Win it! I'm here waiting for you! I hope you don't make me wait for you and I hope you don't say goodbye ever again! I love you too much!

# 32<sup>th</sup> Letter - Unconditional Liar

**23** **August 2010 - 17:50**
You are an unconditional liar and a conditional lover. You say: "Unless you trust me I cannot love you", but, at the same time, you lie, so that means you don't want to be loved.

I believe that to love someone means to accept that person as he or she is, so as I accept that you lie, you should accept that I lost trust on you!

The balance will come with time, as you lie less and I know you better in order to trust you more. For the moment, you should accept things as they are, unless you prefer to use this, among other subjects, as an excuse to refuse love and then cry for something you really don't want, just because you expect the other person to accept something unacceptable.

To love is to accept the differences. I hope you stop seeing us as good and bad, or trust and not trust, or low level and high level! I hope you can see us as just two persons in love!

Put your pride aside and accept your imperfections! Problems are part of life and many relationships live with much more difficult challenges than ours.

We have love while most people have a friendship in their relationship. We have compatibility while most people have agreements. We live as one while others just learn to live together. We understand each other naturally while others have to make efforts all their life.

Love asks for responsibility and commitment and that's why it's so hard to live it. Do you want to talk about levels? Love is the highest one. Only by accepting love, you prove that you're a person in a high level. The higher level is about love, responsibility, commitment and truth.

Look at the people that you fear and see if they have this! They don't.

Love pushes you up but you're afraid to lose yourself. But love is about letting yourself be lost.

I lost myself and I don't regret it because I became someone else in this love, even thought I'm much more myself than before.

Grow up! Accept love! To accept love means to accept happiness, to trust another person, to build hope for the future and improve ourselves by facing our flaws.

You said to me, after I went away, that you don't want to wait another life to meet me, so let's live our dream now! Apart, we will have more fights and, as time passes, we'll be afraid to be together and have fights again, so anyway is a dead end path. This is why I gave up. I still don't know if talking to you again is a good idea but I'll wait for you to show me.

# 33<sup>th</sup> Letter - Read and Assume

## 02 September 2010 - 01:04

I appreciate if you stop making me feel guilty when things don't go as you want either as a lie or something true! It's a tendency that you have that works against you, as I'm able to analyze what kind of efforts you really make and compare them every time you do it.

The person that cares for you, will try to understand, and in this effort, will see your failures, so be careful when you judge me by imposing guilt! You ask too much for things you shouldn't even ask and then you punish like you're superior to me! You aren't and I have the right to disagree with you. So, it's either you learn how to behave or you'll call me mean all your life. I'm not an idiot and I won't close my eyes to your attitudes just because you need it.

After the efforts I did for our relationship to work, I'm now suffering everyday again, this time for being apart with the feeling that you're so afraid to love me that you will try to keep this love at distance for I don't know how much more time.

Distance between us delays whatever you want to have with me and doesn't allow me to see if it can ever be possible.

I don't know what kind of love are you really wishing to have with me and the uncertainty of it works like a toxin in my heart, as I know from your own mouth that this is what you did in the past with the ones that you've abandoned.

I have the right to say how you hurt me and I have the right to feel hurt when you hurt. If you don't respect my feelings and if you don't allow me to express myself, you're searching for something I'm not.

I really don't know what to think when you say: "I just wanted to hear your voice", or, "even if we're not together, I need us to be friends". I wonder if you really want a relationship with me. You have no respect for me and you're playing with me. It's almost a year now, in which you make me feel like a puppet in your hands. But I won't play stupid all my life.

At least, when I talk like this, I'm giving you a chance, as it's in my silence that I give up. And I'm still waiting for your explanation to why you've checked my personal files and copied very private things without my permission from my external hard-drive.

Then you wonder why I don't trust you. Worse than that, you demand my trust while not doing anything to deserve it.

You shouldn't use the love I feel for you against me as you know you give pain in this behavior! If you ask for trust without deserving it, you're asking for my pain and stupidity as to trust you is what I wish the most.

Watching my private files doesn't hurt me as I know since I met you that you're not a trustable person and I take risks all the time to be with you without knowing what you'll do next. It's the fact that you've copied files of my books that hurts me, because I could have given those files to you if you had asked. This attitude means that you don't trust me or my help but you want to steal my knowledge. It makes me feel very sad.

You'll never know me if you try to use what you see, because you see little with a self-destructive intelligence.

In case you want to talk to me, know this: I won't accept the guilt of your attitudes just because you refuse to assume responsibilities concerning your own actions! I can't help you if you're unable to help yourself, so don't ever say again that I'm not helping you as you're the one that refuses my help.

When you think about the relationship in the beginning, remember that you were accepting my help. Those were the good times as you really need to be helped. I connected what was disconnected for a lot of years. Then I helped you face the pain of the past as it controls your conscious mind without you realizing it and therefore making you hurt others when in fact you believe you're just protecting yourself. Besides, even if after that you decided to refuse my help and kept talking to people that I warn you to avoid, you saw later that these people I said to you to be careful about are exactly the ones that have betrayed you when you needed them the most.

Magic isn't enough when the brain doesn't work properly. If you don't believe in it, look at your life! So much endless perfection in so much increasing emptiness.

Remember this: I may be your best chance in life, not with my friendship or my voice, not with my help or reproaches, and not even with my love, but because of the love that you can give to someone that accepts you by loving you. The other way is the way you have been following.

I don't give you so much because I enjoy having pain but because I believe in you. I wish that you would share so much of your life as you ask me to share mine; I wish you were so available to me as you want me to be available to you; I wish you gave so much love and trust as you wish me to give mine.

If you wish to solve your life and find love, face the fact that you're not who you think you are! Face the fact that you're the one killing yourself and not the lack of love in the world, because love sustains the world itself! Face the fact that your true beauty isn't seen by those that admire you but only by those who love you!

If you want to have my respect, assume your failures, prove me when I'm wrong and I'll respect you, but don't judge me if you don't want to be judged yourself! If you don't commit, I don't want you near me because the memories hurt a lot!

The silly thing about this email is that I really need you to read it and understand it but you won't do it or you'll only see little parts of it and then interpret as you wish. But I'm sure that, if you had stolen it from my hard-drive, you would have read it carefully word by word.

In my life, and unless I'm insane...

- I won't marry someone that cannot live with me;
- I won't want to have a son with someone that can't even accept me;
- I won't share a house with someone that struggles to live in secrecy;
- I won't trust someone that steals my knowledge.

We can call this person any name but I'm sure, in all the pain that love can bring when the storm destroys its fruits, that all psychologists, psychiatrists and healthy persons around the world would agree on this. It's not about you, it's about life.

# 34<sup>th</sup> Letter - Maybe

**07** **September 2010 - 10:41**

If you believe that you're superior to me or that I should be punished for being able to see what you do on my back, you're not showing me love. When you find yourself in despair again, for living an empty life without meaning, you'll wish to have love. If love comes to you again, please treasure it as you never did before! Maybe the next man that you'll love has what you couldn't give me: Respect, Compassion and Commitment.

- Maybe, if you weren't so proud of yourself, you could admit your sins and ask for forgiveness;

- Maybe, if you could respect me more, it would be easier to handle our problems;

- Maybe, if you did efforts to live with me without losing not even one day, our relationship would work easily;

- Maybe, if you hadn't done bad things against me in my back, like stealing files, you wouldn't feel the need to hide yourself so much and lose your energy and health in that process;

- Maybe, if you could trust me, I could have helped you easily;

- Maybe, if you had searched the help of a mental health professional, you could have seen that I'm not the one hurting you;

• Maybe, if you could have faced your sins and failures, you could have received redemption in your soul, which would clarify your spirit, allowing you to see the truth;

• Maybe, you could see that I really love you but you will never believe.

Maybe, maybe, maybe,... Maybe we will never know!

If you don't believe in God, believe in the redemption of your soul for the day you'll see what you've despised and lost in this behavior full of pride (one of the seven deadly sins).

# 35<sup>th</sup> Letter - Remember

**07** **September 2010 - 16:04**
Remember my love, when you die, you die alone and, once you're dead, and you see the whole and deep truth, you'll regret everything so much that you'll wish to have the same life you have now, just for another chance to have a relationship with me and try to make it work again.

You've asked me not to wait another lifetime to try to make our love work and now that I gave you another chance, you give me despise. You're a liar! Your life is a big lie! You're an illusion to yourself and others!

Life will give you the hell you ask for in your actions! May God have mercy on your soul because it has been stolen from you! You're not a mean person; you've chosen to be one!

I'm used to people like you but I just didn't expect to love one so much and that is how hell has got me. You want love but you can't love.

# 36<sup>th</sup> Letter - Goodbye

**09** **September 2010 - 08:29**
It's unbelievable how you make efforts to have me back in your life, how you beg for me not to leave you, how you make so many promises and now you leave me to fall again. It's what you enjoy doing: To feel my pain. It's how you feel greater: By sucking my energy through my pain.

You're a coldhearted vampire with no compassion or emotions.

I thought that you have changed but it was all a lie. You'll never change. But yes, you'll always be my little angel, my little fallen angel. You couldn't see my love, my apologies and the dreams I was holding for you, hidden in the last door of my heart, deep in my loving soul.

You ask little from life when you abandon love, and you reject the real joy of living when you reject a true lover. You cannot see love when is too big for your eyes!

In your moments of agony, when you call me one thousand times a day, do you really miss me or you just need a replacement for your loneliness? Do you really cry tears of hope and love when you think of me or you're just afraid to face the consequences of your own decisions and then you need to block the power of your conscience in the acknowledgement of despising love?

The fact that you would abandon me one day like you're doing now was predictable but, in my love for you, I gave my life and switched off my awareness. I gave myself to you with love!

In your moments of agony, alone with your mind, it will all become clear and you'll suffer the power of conscience! When that happens, your heart will suffer for what you made yourself lose!

None of the people that have supported your decision now, will be able to take away that pain. The pain of losing true love. You'll have it on your own, until your dying days. And when you lay down with the next man in your life, you'll not feel the same that you felt with me, and because you cannot erase that fact, you'll feel even bitterer and more sorrowed. In your pain, you'll erase even more the capability to have a clear conscience, you'll erase feelings and you may get some diseases back!

I've given you the light you needed in your darkness but you're now a creature of the dark; you despise all light and you despise all love and conscious freedom. You hold on to your sins as a life-battery that makes your heart beat without emotions.

Maybe if I've never had given you so much love, so much light, your eyes could see me better in the darkness they only know. The dreams I had for you are now my everyday nightmares. You have taken the last energy in me and I'm today a walking dead. You've taken all my love; you have won! But in the day I saw you for the first time, I knew I had lost already. In the day I said "I love you", I was surrendering.

- If in life you feel a pain higher than the one that made you gave up on me, remember that it's just the pain of the light bringing introspection into your mind, so that you can exorcise your demons;

- If one day you feel the pain of dying, remember that it's just God exorcising you through your sins and taking your soul back to him;

- If one day in life you end up alone in a room, with no husband, no children and no joys to share with, remember, my little angel, love was always there, and everywhere, and it came to you in the past in the form of a living man;

And,

- If in life you wish to die, remember, my little angel, that it's just the lack of love, not of the world, but yourself! Remember that you had it and in this agony of pleasant memories you'll exorcise yourself into the light!

# 37<sup>th</sup> Letter - I Wish...

**10** **September 2010 -13:30**
I wish you could say "I'm sorry" when I point your mistakes because I would triple my affection and respect towards you and you would heal my wounds and allow me to keep loving you easily! I also wish you could allow me to say I'm sorry because, every time I hurt you, I'm really sorry, and if you could hear my apologies, instead of sending me away or saying goodbye, you could benefit from the love I would give you to heal your wounds.

I wish we had learned to share more love and less pain because both exist from the strong connection we have!

I confess, as you're afraid that I may know things you hide, I'm afraid I may lose you if you don't show them.

I've lied when I said that I'll take you out of my heart, as I don't want to do that and I don't want to reject emotions. I either feel love or pain for not having you but I'll go till the end on this.

Listen to your heart as it's where love can be found. Your heart will always tell you what the best thing to do is!

# 38<sup>th</sup> Letter - Your Wounds!

**10** **September 2010 - 22:25**
I can't stop loving you and, after all that we had, I know that this love will always be strong and present no matter what happens, no matter where we are or even if we don't see each other again.

I still don't know if it's better to love and lose or to love and let go.

Please heal your wounds and move on with your life in peace. You deserve to be happy. Everyone deserves to be happy and the purpose of life is happiness.

Love should help as it is the strongest and most powerful emotion in the universe. If it doesn't, isn't being lived in the way it should.

You should seek to live the love that embraces you higher! And I'm sorry not to have been good enough to allow you this experience and fulfillment! I'm not a mean person but I've done mean things out of my pain. Forgive me as I never wanted to hurt you! I hope you keep believing in love! I couldn't understand how to love you but I felt it with you like I never felt before.

Please forgive me, forgive yourself and forgive ourselves! If I see you well and loving another man, I'll know I've won because no love was lost.

I will say now what allows me to build an illusion that helps me in hiding this pain from myself; I will say what allows me to blind my heart from the pain of losing love; I will say what permits me to create a dream for my heart to feel the need to keep beating continually; I will say: "See you soon". Because my heart will forever wait for you!

# 39<sup>th</sup> Letter - I Believe

**23** **October 2010 - 18:30**
I believe in dreams...

Because I've dreamed about you all my life without knowing if you existed and life has proven me that you are real.

I believe in fairytales...

Because I thought that my own beliefs where a personal illusion that allows me to build a life with but you've proven me that together we can bring our mutual magic beliefs into reality. With you I've lived all the magic I could wish for!

I believe in vampires...

Because I was seduced by you and felt embraced in your smell and touch but you've sucked all my energy trough pain and guilt. Because, in this hell, I've wished and still wish to die, just to keep the emotion I became addicted to: Loving you!

# 40<sup>th</sup> Letter - Burn in Hell!

**16** **January 2015 - 18:18**
You are cruel, you're a demon in this world. You've runaway after everything that you've done. But I hope that you pay for everything that you've done to me and others, and burn in hell for all eternity!

After more than 39 letters, you searched for me, when I was mourning our breakup and learning to forget you. You found me, you found where I was, you found my building and even my door, and you surprised me in one morning. But what for?

You came to me like a wreck, with old clothes and shoes with wholes, full of excuses about how much you were vomiting and in pain for our breakup, telling me how you had gone back to your alcohol addiction again because you didn't had me anymore.

What other choice did I truly have to believe why someone would surprise me like that? I did what a man should do: I fucked you more than 20 times in one day, and then dumped you in the next. But you behaved like you deserved it, and you kept claiming for my love. And so, I gave you, what I guess was the trillion chance in less than one year, to prove your unworthiness.

When I went to visit you back in your city and stay in your place for Christmas in 2010, I took an airplane to be with you. And then your soul showed me what your demons couldn't. You asked me to watch a movie, which, according to you, reminded you a lot of me. In that movie, the main character, a stupid and retarded man, had sex with a woman that was a complete whore and even fucked other men in his own house, while he watched TV. Wow! You're really a fucking bitch! But thank you! I guess.

I don't see myself as stupid as that guy portrayed in the movie, but probably most of the times in which I knocked at your door and you replied for me to go away, you were having sex with someone else, and then, when they didn't gave a shit about you, you would call me in despair. Because, let's face it, when you asked me during our first two weeks together: "Would you like to have an open relationship with me", you had everything planned already. It wasn't a test! I was just one more in your immense collection. And you got paranoid every time you saw me with my Spanish friends, because they were part of the gang bang, wasn't it?

I was so screwed in my brain due to this relationship, that I ended up searching for the help of two fortunetellers and three psychiatrists. I described them the whole situation, and even shared with them your picture and letters. It was thanks to them, and my friends, that I got a punch in the stomach so hard that I couldn't breathe well for a long time. I had to do jogging five times a day and for several months to get over it and deal with the excruciating and endless pain you left me with.

They saw everything, but you know how I am, and you know how blindly in love I was! I just couldn't see the obvious! So I had to pay several hackers and even a spy company to get the truth from the hell I was living in. And I finally got it, the whole truth. This is what they found about you: You are a nymphomaniac and a schizophrenic. So, when you told me that one of your ex-boyfriends was a psychologist that locked you in his house, you were referring to the mental hospital where your mother has put you and from where you runaway from, wasn't it? Did you fuck the psychologist to get the exit key? Is that why you call him ex-boyfriend? It is, isn't it?

You're an expert thief, and you've learned a lot during those years in which you runaway from a psychiatric hospital in France to travel to England as a young and very sick girl, to become an escort there. That's why you told me that life in England is very difficult, despite the fact that you were making tons of money just for being young and beautiful, as you mentioned in your own words.

I still wonder if you really worked in a porn shop during those years, as you said you did, or even a perfume company as a seller. Because I got access to your fake diplomas from college, and understand now why you told me that I could fake one easily to get a higher salary. And so, the most likely thing that you did in England, especially taking into account that you told me that you were making easy money and living a luxurious life, was being a well-paid VIP Prostitute. That's how you really visited so many different hotels, as you told me. And I bet that, many times, in which you disappeared from me, you were going to suck some stranger's cock in enhance for money and peace of mind, wasn't it? You're as addicted to sex as you are in need for it and the psychological benefits that it brings you.

You used to wake up at 6 o'clock every morning, while I was still sleeping, and then you would continuously and nervously check if I would wake up and see what you were doing, which was creating profiles online to find clients.

I never thought that such people exist in the world. I've seen horror movies and spy movies, and nothing could prepare me for what I experienced with you.

When we were sleeping together, I had lots of nightmares, and you told me that it was your mother making some kind of spell, because she's a professional witch. But I know now that this isn't true. Besides, why would your mother create spells on me, if I'm christian? It was the demon inside you doing this, to weaken me and make me more vulnerable.

None of the people I talked to about you dared to say that you're possessed by a demon, but I read many books about it, lived with you, and slept with you, and can confirm that you match every single trait of the perfectly possessed individuals.

What did they told me and found is that you have sex with many men at the same time, just like in the movie that you've shown me at your place. So thank you for that!

They also saw that you're a thief and a filthy whore, even though these are my own words, as I believe they synthesize your profile much better.

The most unbelievable thing in all this story is that, when I finally kicked you out of my life, you didn't left. You made me pay for an airplane ticket for you to leave my new apartment, and that you never paid back, and that ticket cost me nearly one thousand dollars. I paid for you to go away as fast as possible, and because you told me that you were broke.

Nevertheless, instead of going away normally, you had to take your revenge one last time. You copied all my files from the computer again. But now you did more than that as well. You stole things from my house and even money, and you runaway in a moment in which I was out of the house.

I allowed you to sleep in my house until you were gone of my life, but you planned everything very well, and made me regret not having done what everyone told me to do, which was to throw your things out of the window and call the police to put you out of my apartment.

Even though you managed to escape in a horrible way, I did got a chance to use the police on you, as you had stolen things from me. At the airport, I had a team of police officers ready to guide me to you and stop you from boarding the plane. But you know what? In the exact last second, I was actually happy that you were gone, and decided that I didn't want to stop you from catching that plane. I told them to cancel the operation!

You're a filthy whore and a very ugly human being, if there's still anything human in you. Yes, you're nothing more than a stinky trashcan as you used to call yourself when I met you. And I'm amazed to know that you got a chance to go to Switzerland and clean your record from your disgraceful past once again. Yes, I do know where you are. I also know that you keep escaping your evilness, by not posting your pictures on online profiles, and by changing your name whenever you need. You keep fooling half the world with your new jobs and fake profiles while escaping the other half.

Now, thanks to meeting me, you got all the knowledge needed to have the life that you never deserved to have. I helped you change your entire life for the first time, and become rich like you never were. And what did you gave back to the only person that has given you what you've never deserved, a second chance in your darkness? Nothing! You didn't even confess everything that I paid to find about you. And not even when I got all the proves and access to your email box, and begged for a confession, not even then, you confessed everything. Because you are cruel and ruthless!

I don't deserve to have suffered so much pain. I ruined my health because of you. And I don't know how many sexual diseases I may have gotten through you.

You used me because I was in love with you. You tried to destroy me because I tried to save you. You tried to send my soul to hell because I tried to take yours from it. Filthy creature from hell!

I rest my soul today knowing that you will burn in hell.

# Book Review Request

Dear Reader, Thank you for purchasing this book! I would love to know your opinion. Writing a book review helps in understanding readers and also has an impact on other reader's purchasing decisions. Your opinion matters. Please write a book review! Your kindness is greatly appreciated!

# Booklist

Books written by the author:
Agne: Inside the Mind of a Narcissist
Destiny: When Your Soulmate Finds You
Disenchanted: Poems by Rowan Knight
Illusion: When a Nymphomaniac Falls in Love
One Chance: 20 Short Stories with a Plot Twist and Moral Lesson
Prophecy: A Message to Humanity
Slave: Fulfilling a Prophecy
Soulless: Letters to a Narcissist

# About the Publisher

This book was published by the 22 Lions Bookstore.
For more books like this visit www.22Lions.com.
Join us on social media at:
Fb.com/22Lions;
Twitter.com/22lionsbookshop;
Instagram.com/22lionsbookshop;
Pinterest.com/22LionsBookshop.